MAIN SENSOR RECTENNA

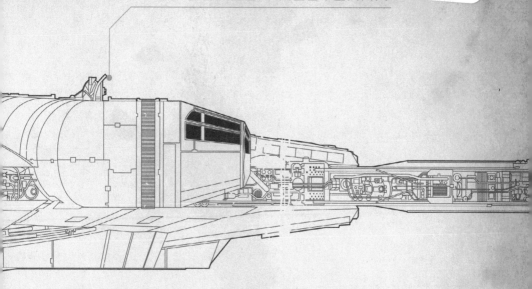

COCKPIT

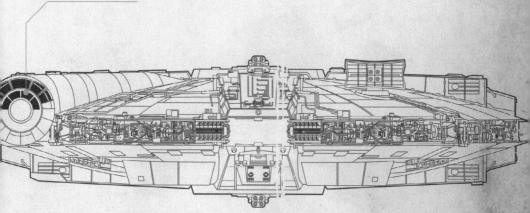

SOLO

A STAR WARS STORY

TALES FROM VANDOR

JASON FRY

studio fun
INTERNATIONAL

"HOWDY, FRIEND. Welcome to Vandor. This here is The Lodge and my name's Midnight. Now that we've been introduced, what can I do for you?"

That's the first thing you'll hear from me when we meet, and the first thing I'll try to find out about you: What do you want?

Something to eat or drink? I can help with that, no matter what planet you come from. (Seriously, try and stump me. You can't.) But let's make one thing clear: don't ask what Iridium Mountain Gorg Eggs really are unless you actually want to know.

Once I know what you want, then I try to find out what you need. If you're thinking those are the same things, let me tell you, they're not. Sometimes folks don't want to admit what they need. Other times they haven't figured it out yet. That's all right, though: helping people find out what they need is part of my job, too.

You might need a game of **sabacc**, or a freighter captain who won't ask questions about what she's hauling, or maybe you need to meet someone involved in the kind of business you don't want to tell the Empire about. Talk to me a little while, and if you seem like a decent sort I'll do what I can.

But listen up, friend, because this next part's important: I can't guarantee things will come out the way you want them to. There's no power in the galaxy that can do that, no matter who you are or how many credits you have. But I can get you pointed in the right direction and maybe give you a little push.

THE LODGE

Once we've taken care of what you want and what you need, the rest is up to you. My favorite nights are  when a stranger walks into the **Lodge** with a story to tell, and all they need is a friendly ear. That's why I started this little book of mine: I wanted to pass on some of the stories I've heard and tell you about the people behind them.

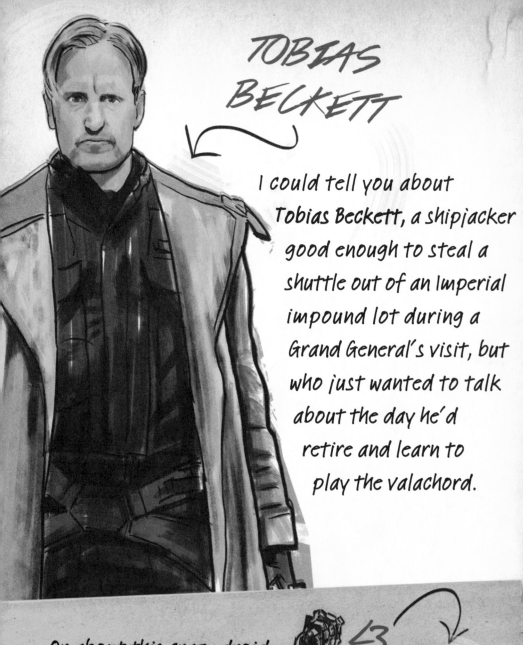

TOBIAS BECKETT

I could tell you about Tobias Beckett, a shipjacker good enough to steal a shuttle out of an Imperial impound lot during a Grand General's visit, but who just wanted to talk about the day he'd retire and learn to play the valachord.

Or about this crazy droid named L3-37 who tried to convince everyone she met that they should fight for droid rights.

L3

Wait 'til you hear about **Lando Calrissian** — he is a real piece of work. When I met him he couldn't fly and wouldn't fight, but he insisted that as long as he sounded good and looked better that everything would work out in his favor.

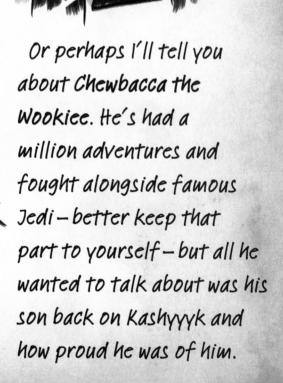

LANDO

Or perhaps I'll tell you about **Chewbacca the Wookiee**. He's had a million adventures and fought alongside famous Jedi — better keep that part to yourself — but all he wanted to talk about was his son back on Kashyyyk and how proud he was of him.

CHEWIE

And wait till you hear about this kid named Han Solo. He might be my favorite, and it's not just because he's a fellow Corellian. (Though, I'll admit, it helps.) Maybe you know Han as the smuggler who runs around with Chewbacca, the one who's run goods all over the galaxy, gotten into trouble with half the crime syndicates, and had his share of scrapes with the Empire.

But when I met him, none of that had happened yet.

When Han first walked into the Lodge he was just a kid, and I'd seen lots of kids like him: smart enough to see trouble coming, but dumb enough to think they could escape it. Most of those kids make a mistake and wind up forgotten by everybody except sentimental old fools like me. I figured Han would be another one of them. I'm glad I've been wrong about that so far.

Yes, I definitely need to tell you about Han and Lando and Chewie and Beckett. But here's the thing, friend: I can't promise that every story I've recorded here is true. I know some of them are, because I was there. But with some of the other stories, let's just say the truth may have gotten stretched a little in the telling.

Then again, sometimes those stories are the ones that are the most fun to hear.

They call me **Midnight** because I've worked a lot of them. And I've learned everybody's got a story that they want to share. Soldiers and scientists have stories, but so do smugglers and swindlers. We get a lot of folks in the Lodge who walk on the wrong side of the law—heck, lots of nights we don't get anybody else. I won't lend those folks credits, but I'll listen to their stories, and maybe trade them one of mine in return. And if you ever visit Vandor, I'll have a seat waiting for you so you can tell me one of yours.

THE ROAD TO VANDOR

It's a big galaxy, sure.

But it used to feel A LOT BIGGER.

I grew up on Corellia, in one of Coronet City's overcrowded favelas. I wasn't called Midnight then, of course. I had a birth name, but I left it behind with everything else.

I wasn't an orphan. I never had to run with one of the shipyard rings or a sewer gang for protection. But my working-class neighborhood never got any attention from the authorities, or credits that might have made our lives better.

It was tough on the best days and downright dangerous on the rest of them. We had too many mouths to feed and too few credits to buy enough food. I saw that the best I could hope for was to grow up and get old and develop Shipbreaker's Cough like my old man. I knew I'd never have clean clothes because of all the soot in the air. And that I'd spend every day working for credits and every night worrying that I didn't have enough of them.

I wasn't going to do it, friend. I couldn't do it. So I saved what I could, signed up to work for passage aboard a bulk freighter, the *Rampaea Horizon*, and left Corellia behind.

I felt better the minute we cleared that old planet's atmosphere. I had to work off the price of my ticket, of course, which took me longer than I would have liked. But once I had, the next choice was mine: I could keep working on the freighter and earn wages or pick a planet and stay on the ground for a while.

So I spent every night in my bunk with an old datapad, looking up information about wherever the freighter was headed next.

Venustria? Too cold.

Ulness Prime? No greenery.

Great Aglamerti? No air.

Funny thing was, I didn't do any research about Vandor. I'd never even heard of it. But the moment the Horizon touched down, I knew this was it. This was home. You could breathe on Vandor, for one thing—real air, without the stink of thruster oil or degreasing salve or that burnt smell left by ion engines. And the sky seemed gigantic out here—it went on forever, above the Iridium Mountains capped with snow. White snow. When it snowed back in Coronet City the flakes were copper-colored before they even hit the ground.

ᔕᘛᗞ᠐᠑ᒎᒎᐯᒪᐱᐯ
ᐯᒪᐱᗞᗞᐱᒪᗺᐱᒎᗞ

INSPECTI

[Emigrants, crew and

Port of Departure: .... Coronet City ....

Name of starship: .... Rampaea Horizon ......

Name of passenger: .... T~~hagerman~~ ....

Security/hygiene inspection at   Port of emba

.... Coronet City ....   Spaceport: ...... Co

DPMAF - DPF		2 2 0
[seal/stamp of local authority]		
02 09 99 3 2 54 4		
CLAS.	DOC.	

Planet: ...... V.

Sector: 3

[The following to be filled in by starship's surge

Ship's list or manifest .... 56 ....

Berth No.   Starship inspection   Days in transit

..... CREW N/A 1 2 3 4 5 6 7 8

ON CARD

[steerage passengers]

Date of Departure: 58-16 (local)

Port of Origin: Corellia

Last Residence: Coronet City

rkation | Items in possession

ulbani | personal gear

ndor

loo

[customs stamp]
A1235A...
CLEARED
SIGNED...

n or authorized agent prior to/after embarkation]

Number on ship's list or manifest 63

CREW N/A

To be completed by surgeon/agent as part of daily inspection

I collected my wages, got my bag, walked off the Horizon, and never looked back.

IRIDIUM
MOUNTAINS

VANDOR

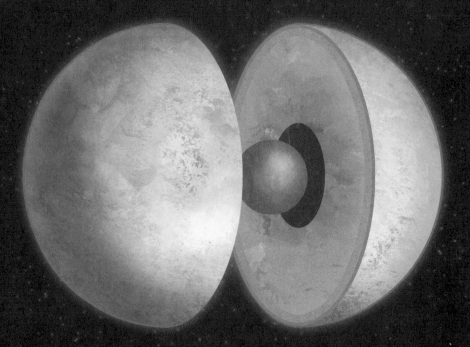

SCOUT SERVICE PLANET ID 53-80 AKA VANDOR IS A TERRESTRIAL WORLD WHOSE CHARACTERISTICS FALL WITHIN ACCEPTABLE PARAMETERS FOR HUMAN HABITATION. PRELIMARY SURVEY REVEALS NO INDIGENOUS SENTIENT LIFE OR SIGNIFICANT ENVIRONMENTAL HAZARDS THAT WOULD IMPERIL SETTLEMENT.

PLANETARY RESOURCES ARE WORTHY OF FURTHER EXPLORATION BY SPECIALIST TEAM. COMPOSITION OF CRUST AND EVIDENCE OF GEOLOGIC UPLIFT SUGGESTS EXTENSIVE MINERAL DEPOSITS MAY BE PRESENT.

FOR NAVIGATIONAL PURPOSES, VANDOR IS RELATIVELY CLOSE TO THE SECONDARY HYPERSPACE ROUTE KNOWN AS THE GAMOR RUN. HOWEVER, THE GRAVITATIONAL SINK KNOWN LOCALLY AS THE LORAHNS CAVITY IS A CLASS-3 NAVIGATIONAL HAZARD, WHILE THE LESSER SLOO GAS CLOUD IS A CLASS-4 NAVIGATIONAL HAZARD. BOTH HAZARDS WILL COMPLICATE TRAVEL IN THE VICINITY OF VANDOR, AND REGULAR UPDATES TO NAVIGATIONAL DATABASES WILL BE REQUIRED FOR TRAVELERS AT A SPACEPORT THAT MEETS BUREAU OF SHIPS AND SERVICES (BOSS) STANDARDS.

PUBLIC SCOUT ARHUL
FOLLOWS.

VANDOR

PLANETARY FILE

GALACTIC REGION: MID RIM

DIAMETER: 12,500 KM

PRINCIPAL TERRAIN: PLAINS, MOUNTAINS

NUMBER OF MOONS: 2

LENGTH OF YEAR: 435 DAYS

POPULATION: UNAVAILABLE

XTENSIVE HERDS OF NON-SENTIENT QUADRU-
EDS ARE ALSO PRESENT AND MAY HAVE
CONOMIC VALUE. SEE FULL WORLD LOG FOR
URTHER DETAILS OF FLORA AND FAUNA. SEE
RELIMINARY SURVEY FOR DETAILS OF OTHER
-SYSTEM WORLDS.

AS A SECONDARY CONSIDERATION, VANDOR'S
UNDISTURBED ECOSYSTEM, EXTENSIVE
MOUNTAIN RANGES AND FAST-FLOWING RIVERS
SUGGEST POTENTIAL VALUE AS A TOURIST
DESTINATION. OUTLYING FRONTIER WORLDS
WITH SIMILAR CHARACTERISTICS (FARHAVA
BETA, GAMERONG, EDIS VII) HAVE BEEN PROFIT-
ABLY EXPLOITED BY CORPORATE INTERESTS.

RELIMINARY CONCLUSION IS THAT THESE NAVI-
ATIONAL DISRUPTIONS ARE THE BIGGEST
EGATIVE FACTOR IN ASSESSING THE ECONOMIC
ALUE OF VANDOR FOR DEVELOPMENT AND/OR
ETTLEMENT. FURTHER SURVEYS RECOM-
ENDED.

STATUS: WORLD LOG AND SURVEYS FILED WITH
REPUBLIC SURVEY CORPS.

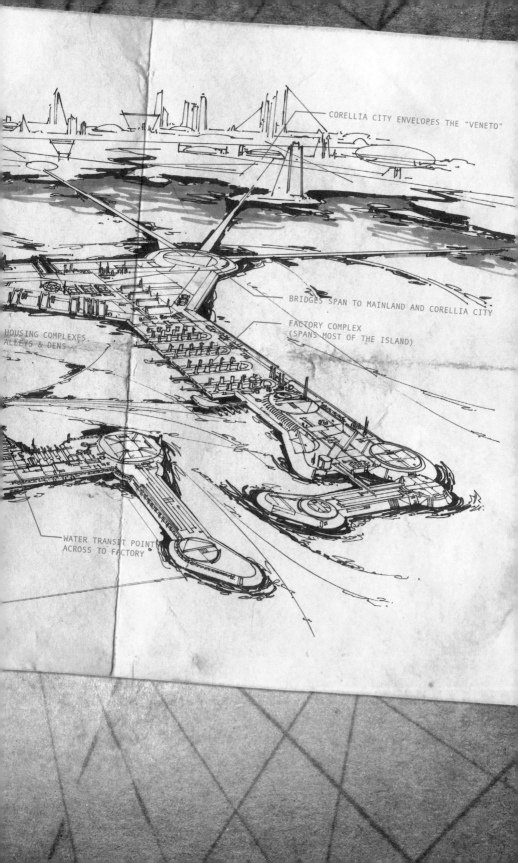

CORELLIA CITY ENVELOPES THE "VENETO"

BRIDGES SPAN TO MAINLAND AND CORELLIA CITY

FACTORY COMPLEX
(SPANS MOST OF THE ISLAND)

HOUSING COMPLEXES,
ALLEYS & DENS

WATER TRANSIT POINT
ACROSS TO FACTORY

KOD'YOK HERDS

How'd I end up at the Lodge? Sooner or later, everyone who comes to Vandor winds up here. There aren't that many other places to go.

I did a little bit of everything to earn a living. First I rode a speeder bike as part of kod'yok roundups, and I learned how to use a skinner's laser knife. I regret that job now that the kod'yok herds are so thinned out.

Then I climbed Big Rock to help set up a comm repeater. And after the Empire showed up, I risked my neck to lay conveyex track across the territory of the Spinnaker Raiders. The Spinnakers are gone now—the last of them joined Enfys Nest's Cloud-Riders when that outfit started recruiting—but back in the day they were a terror.

We had to lay that conveyex track three times. The first two times, the raiders tore up everything we'd done after we moved on. The third time we came around, the Spinnakers didn't wait for us to move on before expressing their displeasure.

CONVEYEX

I was the only one on my work crew to survive the attack—I wrapped myself in a kod'yok skin, held my breath and tried to look small.

I lived, but almost died walking back along the track to base camp:

a TIE fighter on patrol mistook me for a raider and tried to stitch me with his blaster cannons. Thank the stars he wasn't a better shot.

After all those jobs, I'd wind up back at Fort Ypso and visit the Lodge. People come here to hire new workers, to stock up on supplies, and to spend a few credits when they have them. I'd walk in with the skinners and tracklayers and mountaineers, but I stayed away from the card tables — it's hard to calculate proper odds when you're hungry. All I wanted was a meal — a kod'yok steak and some roasted giblins, if I had my druthers — and a quiet place to lay my head until morning.

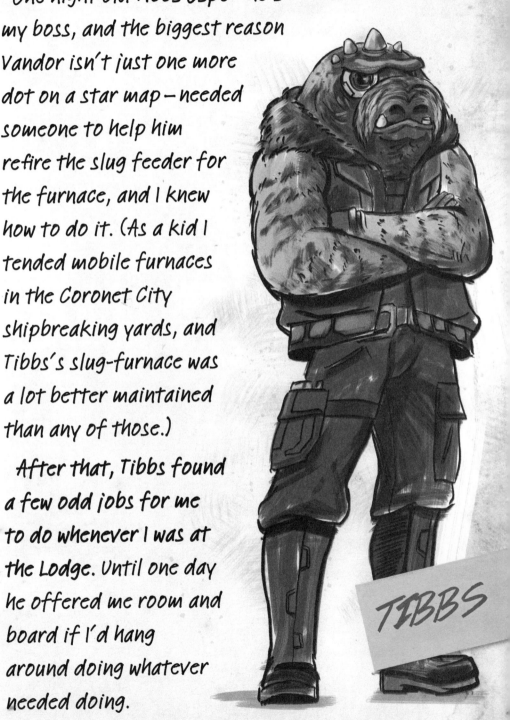

One night old Tibbs Ospe—he's my boss, and the biggest reason Vandor isn't just one more dot on a star map—needed someone to help him refire the slug feeder for the furnace, and I knew how to do it. (As a kid I tended mobile furnaces in the Coronet City shipbreaking yards, and Tibbs's slug-furnace was a lot better maintained than any of those.)

After that, Tibbs found a few odd jobs for me to do whenever I was at the Lodge. Until one day he offered me room and board if I'd hang around doing whatever needed doing.

TIBBS

Tibbs doesn't like to talk much, but over the years I've learned his story. He was a Commerce Guild scout back before the droid war, flying a Vangaard Pathfinder out beyond the Void of Chopani in search of valuable new planets.

That's how he found Vandor, tucked away in an ancient scout's report. It was settled centuries ago, but turned out to be too far from the main trade routes to prosper. So after a couple of generations most of the settlers packed up and looked for a new home.

Tibbs saw things had changed and thought Vandor might make for a good stopping place for traders heading toward Deneba and Manda. So he fixed up the ruins of the old Ypsobay Trading Company headquarters, filled in the craters in the old landing strip, and let folks know they could find food and fuel at Fort Ypso.

And if they needed a place to spend the night or blow off a little steam, they could visit the Lodge.

His old buddies in the scouting service thought he was crazy, but people came, and kept coming back. More of them than Tibbs had really wanted, to be honest, but that's life. Once you start something moving, you don't always get to say how far it will go.

Anyway, I was talking about the day Tibbs offered me a job. His offer sounded good to me—one of my arms was wrapped in bacta tape, flash-cooked from the near-miss with that TIE, and I'd seen too many Spinnaker Raiders up close to want to go back to a conveyex crew.

After all that, I was ready to work inside for a change. So I became Tibbs's chief tinkerer, maintenance guy, carpenter, errand boy and all-purpose helper.

One night a party of skinners came in just as the 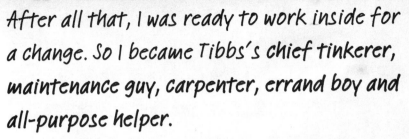 last barkeep went off-shift, so I stayed up to keep them fed and watered. Tibbs listened in, heard I had the gift of gab, and the next morning he told me the overnight job was mine if I wanted it.

If my first night on the job was easy, the second night let me know what I was in for....

There's a Kerestian hunter named Iothene Jacontro who visits Vandor every year or so. These days Jacontro's obsessed with tracking down a vastadon that he swears lives up on the Jirree Glacier, but the first time he came to Vandor he was looking for treasure — specifically, the fabled Corubalni Hoard.

Jacontro showed up with a pack of aliens and told everybody that he'd released wampas into the outback as trophies for a big-game hunt. But the first night — about an hour into my shift — Jacontro's gang started a fight in the hall with the Valarine School, the meanest bunch of Selkath pirates this side of Eriadu.

✗ DEADBEATS
✗ SWINDLERS
✗ LIARS
✗ THIEVES

It went about as well as you'd expect, so the next morning Jacontro came down to find not only an enormous bar bill (and an even bigger bill for damages), but also that half of his gang was dead and the other half was in the lockup down the hill.

Not the best start to a safari, but it got worse. It generally does, friend.

Jacontro needed a new crew, and wound up hiring half of Vandor's deadbeats, swindlers, liars, and thieves. Then they all trooped out of here looking for the Corubalni Hoard. Which I tried to tell them didn't exist, but Jacontro wasn't interested in the opinion of an overnight barkeep.

We figured that the story about the wampas was just cover for the treasure hunt, at least until Tibbs's kod'yoks got devoured.

Jacontro had released wampas all right, but his people had turned them loose right on the other side of the ridge!

While his crew went off hunting for treasure, those ice creatures followed their noses back to Fort Ypso and started wrecking stuff. So now we had wampas attacking convoys and tearing apart cabins, and nobody to hunt them.

Tibbs organized a shooting party, but I decided to sit that one out: I figured I'd stay where it was warm and there was no chance something with claws like razors would try to remove my face.

While Tibbs and the others were bagging wampas, Jacontro had somehow lost his whole gang without finding any treasure. With one arm nearly frozen solid, Jacontro decided he'd had enough of treasure hunting. But on the trek back to Fort Ypso one of the wampas caught his scent. So as Jacontro was settling his debts, a bull wampa busted right through a wall!

Tibbs walked in just in time, raised his rifle and fired one shot to take care of the problem.

At least we got a few decorations out of it—Tibbs had the wampa's arms stuffed and mounted in the back room. And Jacontro couldn't stop Tibbs from giving the name "Iothene's Den" to the room where it all happened.

Anyway, that was my welcome to working nights at the Lodge. At least I knew I wouldn't be bored.

THE GALACTIC
UNDERWORLD

Believe it or not, wampas aren't the worst things in this galaxy. There are all sorts of bad gangs and crime syndicates out there, fighting for power and control.

Of course, the biggest, baddest gang of all is the Empire. The Imperials have the firepower, control the credits, and have shown world after world that getting in their way is a fatal mistake. They mostly stay away from Fort Ypso—they know that out here, hiring a lone bounty hunter is a better way to take care of a problem than sending in a squad of stormtroopers.

Occasionally we get an adventurous officer in here, but they're given the cold shoulder. Usually they get the hint and hit the bricks once their glass is empty or their plate's clean. Which is for the best: there's too many people here at the Lodge whose scandocs come with arrest warrants.

UNITE

IMPERIAL
DOMINATION

JOIN TODAY

I don't like the Empire, but don't go thinking I'm a rebel. I don't like it because it's what I ran away from on Corellia. It's a machine that turns people and places into credits, leaving the grass dead and the air polluted and the sea empty.

The machine doesn't do those things because it's evil, but because that's what it was designed to do. And it's happening on Vandor now too. The kod'yok herds are thinned out by hunting and fences. The mountains are getting blasted apart for iridium. Imperial garrisons and operating bases and towns are springing up along the conveyex line. I guess the loss of the coaxium was a wake-up call for the Empire — and Vandor has paid the price.

In a couple of generations Vandor will be just another planet and someone will have bought the Lodge and turned it into one of those terrible tourist cantinas. I just hope that some old-timer will still remember Midnight.

ᴌᴏᴊᴠᴉ� ᴊ1ᴙ1ᴎᴏᴎ
ᴋᴊᴏᴏᴏᴙ ᴊ

MEDICAL

Only you can prevent lungfung! Keep your respirator mask on unless inside a positively pressurized structure. Imperial mobile surgical units are at capacity and no slots for lung cleanses are available.

The increased ionic activity in the atmosphere will likely be accompanied by higher temperatures and humidity. Maintain proper hydration at all times!

DO NOT drink water unless you know it's imported and has been purified. Filtration of vaporator water is insufficient for eliminating microbes from local sources.

Keep your feet dry! Trench foot provides another opportunity for microbial infection.

5405255805031383

EQUIPMENT

Except during combat operations, transportation of mining equipment is prioritized over all other action items.

Respirator masks and breathing tubes are ineffective if not kept clean. Replace your filters according to the schedule and instructions in your manual.

Additional chemical glow rods are available for E-10 rifles. If you lack one, check in with your quartermaster.

Personnel are responsible for keeping slicks, armor and body gloves free of mud. Muddy equipment makes it difficult for scanners to differentiate hostiles and friendlies.

Atmospheric ionization is impairing com-scan equipment. Weatherproofing efforts continue. Further updates will be provided as they become available.

8168124117133054

ᕟᕟᕼᕟᗡ ᐯᒐᗡᐯᒥᕟᐱᐯᒐ ᗡᕼᕟᕟ
ᐯᒐᕟᕼᕟᐯᗡᕟ ᕼᒐᕟᕼ

TACTICAL

Anti-insurgent operations continue on all fronts in the disputed wilderness zone. Local population continues to resist pacification by ambushing infantry and support personnel, destroying equipment and interfering with mining operations.

Despite their primitive culture, the native Mimbanese are capable fighters with extensive knowledge of our tactics and equipment. They use thatch and insulating mud to obscure heat signatures and foil sensor scans, and set up ambushes with improvised explosives, tripwires and other booby traps. NEVER ASSUME a lack of sensor contact with the enemy means you are in a non-combat situation.

Atmospheric ion storms are forecast to increase in severity. This will make sensor scans less reliable and hamper air support.

9702804111061579

REGULATIONS

Local non-insurgent natives (AKA Greenies) are not allowed in camp unescorted. They are thieves and suspected of conducting reconnaissance for insurgents.

All personnel are required to support Imperial resource teams engaged in hyperbaride mining operations. Never forget that their work is why we're on this mudball.

During forest clearance, all newly discovered native structures are to be reported to survey teams for further inspection. Crystal outcroppings or exposed mineral veins are priority-one reports.

6608226620101985

For all the Empire says about making the galaxy a "safer" place, Imperials certainly aren't above working with the most dangerous gangs and crime syndicates out there.

Take the Pykes from Kessel for example. They mainly mine spice, but they are also sitting on one of the only sources of astatic coaxium in the galaxy that I'm aware of at least. And that kind of incredibly rare, valuable, and powerful hyperspace fuel is exactly what the Empire needs most.

The Pykes' philosophy is that if the Empire wants coaxium, it can have it—the Pykes will figure out how to help and hope to turn a profit by doing so.

Besides, they make most of their credits from running spice, a business the Empire tolerates so long as things don't get out of control. If they were to fight with the Imperials over coaxium, the Empire would just blockade the trade routes in and out of Kessel, stopping the flow of spice. And no crime syndicate in the galaxy wants that.

Long story short: if the Pykes show up in the Lodge, it either means they're looking for pilots to make a Kessel Run, or one of their pilots skipped out with a shipment and they want to track the bugger down. The first one's easy—I point them to the sabacc game or the droid fights, or wherever the pilots are blowing credits they should be spending on maintenance and fuel. The second one's trouble, and suggests someone will be fighting with someone else soon. Either way, I'm happier when the Pykes leave again.

* Transport **only** in approved core tubes constructed of unreactive metal alloys and glass.

* Core tubes **must be kept stable.** Only transport tubes arrayed in approved core racks.

* Only use storage cases made of reinforced carbonite or other insulating material.

* Verify that datascreens are functional and properly monitoring temperate and kinetic activity.

* Move storage cases only using trolleys or hovercarts. **Do not** transport by hand!

* Properly secure storage cases in starship hold to eliminate jostling or unexpected movement.

* Mark empty core tubes and storage cases and secure them with chains or stasis fields.

---

headaches and respiratory failure. Repeated workplace exposure to UNREFINED COAXIUM vapor may cause formation of deposits in internal organs. Such deposits may achieve critical mass and detonate, causing **injury and/or death.**

Moderate irritant to the eyes, mucous membranes and skin of susceptible species.

TREATMENT MEASURES

Immediately flush eyes/mucuous membranes with species-specific hydration medium. Remove contaminated clothing.

For suspected ingestion of vapor, **do not** induce vomiting given volatility concerns. **Seek immediate treatment** with a medical droid updated to include current industrial-safety protocols.

COAXIUM (UNREFINED)

ᑕᕒᕒᑐᕓᑔᑕ ᑐᑐᑕ ᐱᕒᑐ ᑐᕒᐱ

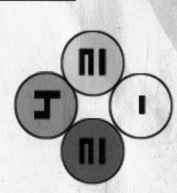

MATERIALS DESCRIPTION

COAXIUM is a highly reactive hypermatter that must be refined for stability and fluidity. In its unrefined state, coaxium is **highly volatile.** Excessive temperature change or jostling during transport may result in detonation.

HAZARDS IDENTIFICATION

Inhalation may cause irritation.

TRANSPORTATION AND HANDLING

* UNREFINED COAXIUM is **highly volatile** and should always be treated as a catastrophic detonation risk. Failure to follow safety protocols will have fatal consequences!

* **Monitor temperature carefully!** UNREFINED COAXIUM is at risk of immediate detonation at a temperature below 35 standard therms. For safety, maintain temperature above 50 standard therms throughout transportation.

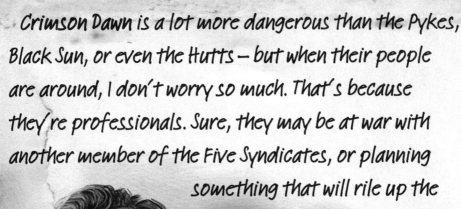

Crimson Dawn is a lot more dangerous than the Pykes, Black Sun, or even the Hutts — but when their people are around, I don't worry so much. That's because they're professionals. Sure, they may be at war with another member of the Five Syndicates, or planning something that will rile up the Empire. But that's syndicate business, and the way Crimson Dawn sees it, civilians who have enough sense to stay out of the way have nothing to worry about.

At least that's the way it has worked out on Vandor.

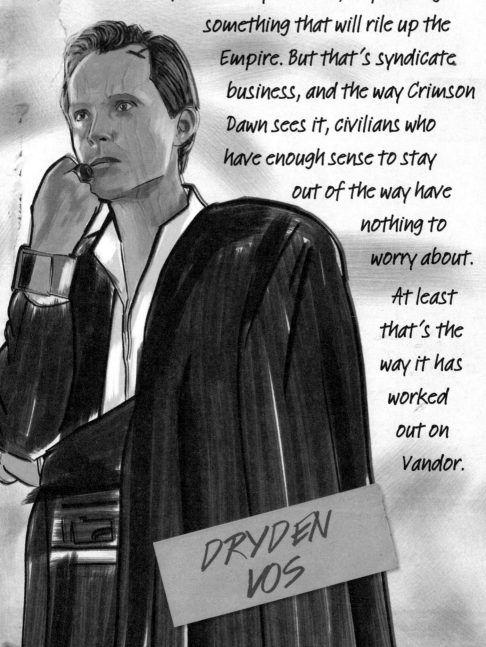

DRYDEN VOS

I've heard stories about other planets that weren't treated as nicely, but then you always hear stories, don't you?

For a while, Dryden Vos — he was one of the big Crimson Dawn bosses — kept his yacht here at Fort Ypso, using it to conduct business. Which meant that lots of folks who'd normally spend credits here in the Lodge were aboard Vos's luxury ship instead. But Vos was a gentleman about it. He'd send his lieutenant, a lady named Qi'ra, to handle any business, he paid his docking fees and fuel charges on time, and he tipped Tibbs generously. That's the Crimson Dawn way as far I've seen, and it's downright neighborly.

Funny thing to say about folks who are criminals and death peddlers, right? I don't disagree, friend. But in this galaxy. I'll take neighborly any way I can get it.

Another gang to watch out for is the **Cloud-Riders.**
They're from the Outer Rim, but they've shown up
on Vandor a few times, and anyone with more than
a spoonful of brains holds his breath when they do.
They keep their faces hidden behind masks, they're
practically dripping with weapons, and they travel in
packs aboard their swoop bikes.

ENFYS
NEST

I hear their home
base is a carrier
ship that never
goes any lower
than the upper
atmosphere,
and the Cloud-
Riders got their
name because they
launch their bikes
right off its deck.
They find a target,
swoop down on it,
and are gone again
almost before you
can blink.

Their leader is a pirate named Enfys Nest, and you hear lots of tales about that name. How Enfys took out the Skyraptors of Unavartan singlehandedly in one night's running fight. How Nest was once a Crimson Dawn lieutenant, and swore a blood oath to eliminate the syndicate to the very last being. How he's really a she, and "Enfys Nest" isn't a name but a title — one only the greatest warriors have a hope of claiming.

I've only seen Enfys once, when the Cloud-Riders came in looking for information and their leader asked for a single drink. (Plain water, if you want to know.) I don't know what's true and what isn't about Enfys, but take my advice: best to whisper that name around here. It's a bad name to hear, and a worse one to say. Because that name attracts attention. And believe me, friend: it's not the kind you want.

'A couple of years back I spent most of one shift talking with a young geology student who had a bad case of hyperlag and couldn't sleep. He looked around at the rough crowd and asked me if I wasn't scared that one night a bunch of gangsters would just take over the place. Now, it wasn't that rough a crowd: but I guess a fancy-pants school like the University of Byblos doesn't prepare you for a spot like ours on Vandor.

I told him that I wasn't worried. Sure, some bunch of gangsters could take over. But then they'd have to run the place. (If you want to get rich, don't open a lodge. It means dealing with inventory, maintenance and lots of other non-heroic stuff, and even when things go well, the profits are small. And crime syndicates are looking for big profits.)

We don't get too many members of the Hutt Cartel visiting. I suppose it's too cold for them. When they do come around, they tend to vanish into private rooms and send their hirelings out to fetch whatever they need. Given that Hutts leave a trail of slime wherever they go, that's no great loss for the rest of us.

Another gang we don't see around here much is the Droid Gotra, probably because Vandor doesn't have enough droids to attract their attention. Still, I hope they never find out about Ralakili's droid fighting ring...

Truth is, I'm sympathetic to the Gotra: it's a hard thing feeling like someone else's property, whether you're flesh and blood or metal and wires. But if I were a mechanical, I figure I'd head to a planet with more reliable recharge centers and oil baths.

HUTT

The way I look at it, friend, everybody's got their secrets – you, me, everybody. It's just that folks coming to the Lodge have more of them.

I've learned to listen for when someone wants to part with a secret that's been troubling them, and when someone wants you to keep your distance. But sometimes people part with their secrets without quite meaning to. You talk with them and a secret comes out, except it comes out sort of sideways.

Beckett and his gang were never regulars, but we'd see them every few months, sniffing around the Empire's operations.

That was when I got to know him, Rio, and Val.

Some folks with less than perfect pasts are suspicious of their own words, as if they might be traps. But Rio was the opposite, a six-armed Ardennian chatterbox who'd fill a room with words because he was afraid of silence. That's a type I've encountered a few times: the comedian whose jokes hide a broken heart. I never did find out what had happened to Rio, but I was always glad to see him and laugh at his stories.

Val was the one to watch on that crew. Man, was she cool under fire.

The first night I met the Beckett gang, some wannabe bounty hunter from a local bandit outfit drew on a Whitescar courier and tried to collect on him. Val was sitting at the bar behind the guy. She leaned forward, popped him in the shoulder so his arm went dead, and plucked the blaster out of his hand. The Lodge had gone dead silent, but Val just turned to the courier and said: "Find a place where nobody knows you, and find it fast."

The courier took off and Val reached back over her shoulder to hand me the blaster. Didn't even look, just knew I was there. She said, "Midnight, hang onto that till this one's learned how to use it." And then she bought the wannabe bounty hunter a drink. That was it. Took me longer to tell the story than it did for it to happen. After that, I knew I never, ever wanted to mess with that lady.

Beckett, though? I never did quite figure him out.

First I heard of him and his gang was after their operation at the Berullian Checkpoint. They spent weeks stealing Imperial supply ships in the Berullian theater of operations, which caused three different Imperial advisors to pitch a fit and the Emperor to dispatch Grand General Ormeddon to clean house. Which was what Beckett wanted. Ormeddon thought he was coming to fix things, and never suspected the thefts were designed to get him away from his security, where he'd be vulnerable. Beckett and the others were waiting at the checkpoint, disguised as maintenance workers. Fifteen minutes into Ormeddon's inspection, they took his shuttle, jumped back to Foundry, used the Grand General's clearance codes to land in his personal docking bay, then stole experimental shield-generator technology. By the time Ormeddon finished his inspection and started asking where his shuttle was, the gang was on the other side of the galaxy arranging a deal with thieves working for the Crymorah syndicate.

Beckett's gang pulled a lot of jobs like that. Fixed up a navigation buoy from Old Republic days and used it to lure an Imperial replenishment fleet into the Llon Shoals, then drained the fuel for resale. Spent three months as wreckers on the fringes of the Celestial Wake, waylaying Mining Guild oreships. The Bhuna Sound Heist? That was them. So was the Mairenhelm Deception.

Navigation Buoy

I never asked Beckett or the others about these jobs – a wise man doesn't let on that he knows any more than he's been told. But I learned Beckett was from Glee Anselm, and what he really wanted to do was get home and learn to play the valachord.

You'd think a hard-bitten thief like Tobias Beckett would be from some harsh planet where you couldn't go outside, but he was from a tropical paradise. And he wanted to sit on the beach and make music. Or at least that's what he said.

I guess he never got to do that, not if the stories about what went down on Savareen are true. And that's a shame. But there's a lesson in that...

Beckett didn't start out wanting to be a shipjacker or a thief. He wanted to play the valachord. But life had other plans. Take it from me, friend—it always does.

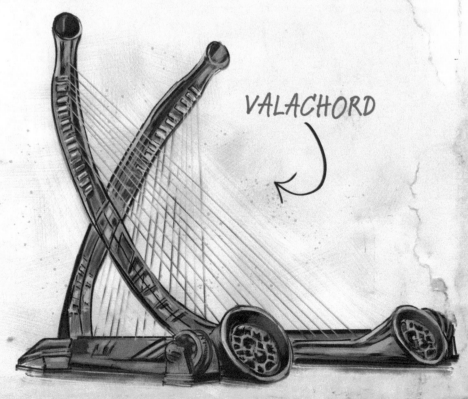

VALACHORD

HAN SOLO

I knew about the Beckett gang, but I never would have guessed that Han Solo would turn out to be its most famous member. When I met Han, I figured he wouldn't live long enough to get off the planet. You see, Beckett's gang had just lost an entire shipment of coaxium that it owed to Crimson Dawn, and word in Fort Ypso was it was young Solo's fault. Han was trying to look brave and tough, but anyone could see he was scared. At least he had that much sense. It was too bad—he was a fellow Corellian, after all.

When he found out I was from Coronet City too, he looked so wary that I knew he must have grown up running with one of the orphan gangs.

I wouldn't have guessed he'd been a scrumrat for the White Worms, though. That impressed me. It takes a lot of gumption to get yourself out of the sewers and away from Lady Proxima, let alone offworld entirely. Han calmed down once he figured out I wasn't interested in collecting any reward the Worms might have out for a runaway. He told me he'd been an Imperial pilot—a great one, he wanted me to know—but now he was a deserter. When I told him that could be a death sentence, he said he knew it, but serving with the Imperial Army on Mimban had been a different kind of death sentence.

LADY PROXIMA

STAR DESTROYER
CONSTRUCTION

Well, that was the second time since Han walked in the door that I realized there was more to him than I'd thought.

It was all starting to make sense. I'd heard the gossip that Beckett and his gang were running a job on Mimban, and now they'd showed up with a Wookiee and a new kid in tow, and the kid was a former mudtrooper.

Believe you me; Han's not the first Corellian to get off world by signing up for Imperial service. Heck, he's not even the millionth and first. Lots of kids choose that way out, particularly now that the Empire has sent so many shipbuilding contracts to Corellian yards.

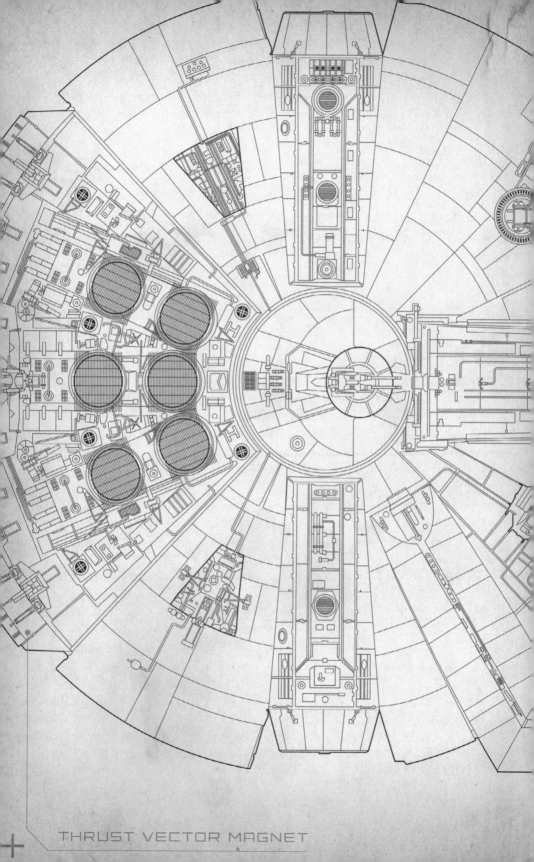

THRUST VECTOR MAGNET

Studio Fun International

An imprint of Printers Row Publishing Group

A division of Readerlink Distribution Services, LLC

10350 Barnes Canyon Road, Suite 100, San Diego, CA 92121

www.studiofun.com

Copyright © & TM 2018 Lucasfilm, Ltd.

Written by Jason Fry

Illustrated by Sam Gilbey

Designed by Tiffany Meador-LaFleur

Cover designed by Andrew Barthelmes

Printers Row Publishing Group is a division of Readerlink Distribution Services, LLC.

Studio Fun International is a registered trademark of Readerlink Distribution Services, LLC.

All notations of errors or omissions should be addressed to Studio Fun International, Editorial Department, at the above address.

ISBN: 978-0-7944-4102-9

Manufactured, printed, and assembled in Stevens Point, WI, United States of America.

First printing, June 2018. WOR/06/18

22 21 20 19 18 1 2 3 4 5

Next time Han comes by the Lodge I'll ask him about all of these things — assuming he's not trailed by bounty hunters, a pack of Gank killers hired by the Hutts, or a squad of stormtroopers.

Wherever his name came from, and whatever he's been up to, it'll make a good story. And the Lodge wouldn't be the Lodge without those, now would it?

On the other hand, a Snivvian bounty hunter was in here one day and swore that while almost everything about Han Solo on the official channels was a lie, his last name really was Solo. He said his research revealed Han was a direct descendant of ancient Corellian royalty—Prince-Admiral Jonashe Solo himself. He claimed the Hutt cartel knows this, and wants to back Han as heir to the long-vacant throne of Corellia.

Then just the other night, this retired Imperial intake officer said the Empire's standard military intake form requires a last name, and the computer system rejects any application if the last name is left blank. So if you come from a culture where people only have one name, joining the Empire means getting a second one whether you like it or not. She said different intake officers fill in different last names, and two of the most common choices are NA — for "not applicable" — and SOLO.

If that's what happened to Han, I guess he's lucky. He could have become known as Han Na.

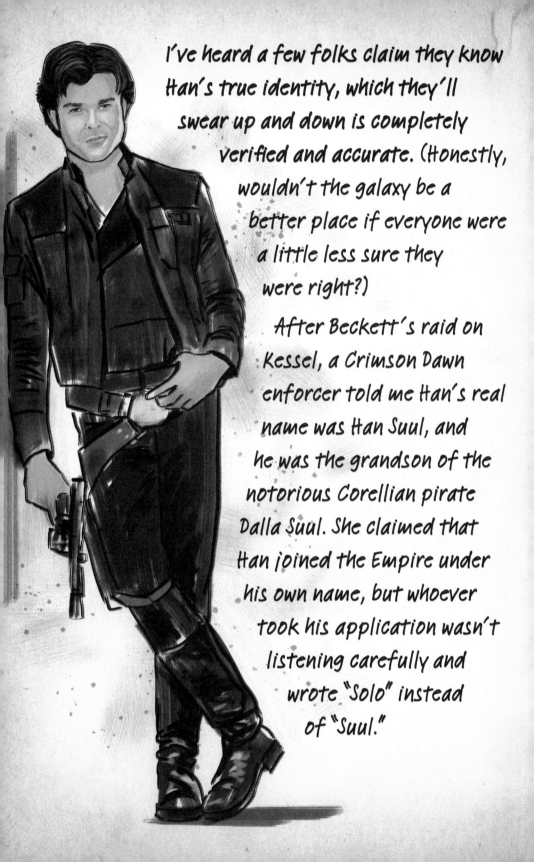

I've heard a few folks claim they know Han's true identity, which they'll swear up and down is completely verified and accurate. (Honestly, wouldn't the galaxy be a better place if everyone were a little less sure they were right?)

After Beckett's raid on Kessel, a Crimson Dawn enforcer told me Han's real name was Han Suul, and he was the grandson of the notorious Corellian pirate Dalla Suul. She claimed that Han joined the Empire under his own name, but whoever took his application wasn't listening carefully and wrote "Solo" instead of "Suul."

I thought I'd hear the Kashyyyk story again, but she told me the story she had heard had happened on Coruscant.

She said Han grew up there, not on Corellia or Kashyyyk, and made a dishonest living by joining youth tours of important landmarks and then stealing from the real tourists. Posing as Ian, he infiltrated the Jedi Temple, only to discover that Separatist agents had attacked the temple to steal battle plans. Han joined Jedi Master Yoda — now there's a name I hadn't heard in a long time — and helped the Jedi and clone troopers recover the plans.

Yes, really. That's really what she said to me. It felt like one of those goofy holo-tales that only works if you're in on the joke from the beginning. But that archaeologist wasn't joking, and she had a question for me: Since Han Solo was working for the Jedi then, how did I know he wasn't still working for them now? Sometimes even I don't know what to say.

THE BOY AT THE JEDI TEMPLE

It's crazy the kinds of stories you hear about Han these days.

An archaeologist came to Vandor in search of an ancient temple she swore was beneath the Jirree Glacier. When you hear "ancient temple" and then the person looks around to see if anyone's listening, you know they're talking about the Jedi. This night no one was listening, so the archaeologist asked if I knew that Han Solo had helped the Jedi as a child.

I never saw Bollux again, so I figured he was just another malfunctioning droid. Until this retired Corporate Sector big shot visited to hunt kod'yok. He was nervous and said he'd used up all his luck cheating death and needed to keep looking over his shoulder. The big shot told me he'd been invited to tour the Corporate Sector's new prison, Stars' End, but had to cancel, which was a lucky break for him considering that the prison got blown into orbit by saboteurs, led by some lowlife Corellian who broke in to free a Wookiee.

Maybe Bollux was telling the truth. If anyone could plan a prison break but wind up accidentally blowing a tower into orbit, it's Han Solo.

A DROID LOOKING FOR *TREASURE*

Speaking of secrets, one night an old labor droid moseyed into the Lodge with a message for Essvee, one that included Han Solo's name.

His name was Bollux, and he said he'd been there when Han blew a Corporate Sector Authority prison off the surface of a planet to rescue Chewie, and helped

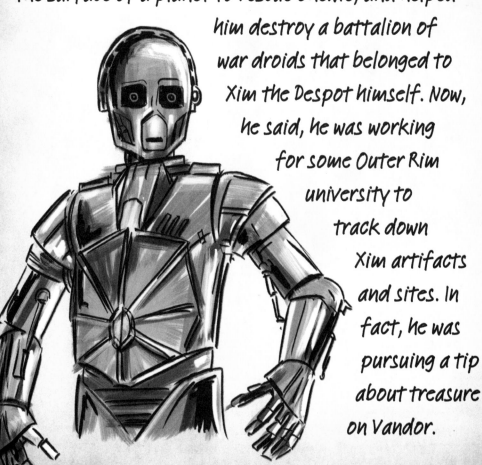

him destroy a battalion of war droids that belonged to Xim the Despot himself. Now, he said, he was working for some Outer Rim university to track down Xim artifacts and sites. In fact, he was pursuing a tip about treasure on Vandor.

There's a loudmouth flyboy named Rendar who swears Chewbacca deserves the real credit, explaining that Wookiee scouts on Kashyyyk know secret routes all over the galaxy, and Chewie shared one of them with Beckett's gang.

And Astrid Fenris insists Han went between a pair of black holes on the outskirts of the Maw, which means the credit really ought to go to Lando for modifying the *Falcon* so that it was tough enough to take that kind of punishment. Fenris swears she'll find Han's route and claim it for her own, except the Maw is full of black holes, and she isn't quite sure which two Han went between. Every time she drops by the Lodge someone asks her if she's gotten up the courage to test her theory, and she takes a sudden interest in another subject – any other subject.

I don't know which explanation is correct and what Han really did– heck, from what I know of Han he may not be entirely sure about that himself. But whatever it is, it'll be recorded in the *Falcon's* logs. Which means it's Han's secret – at least until someone can persuade him to part with it.

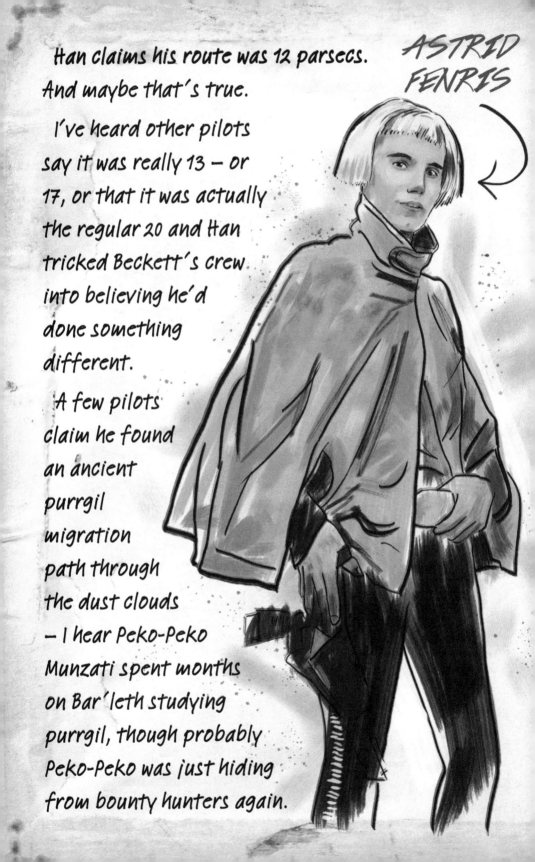

Han claims his route was 12 parsecs. And maybe that's true.

I've heard other pilots say it was really 13 — or 17, or that it was actually the regular 20 and Han tricked Beckett's crew into believing he'd done something different.

A few pilots claim he found an ancient purrgil migration path through the dust clouds — I hear Peko-Peko Munzati spent months on Bar'leth studying purrgil, though probably Peko-Peko was just hiding from bounty hunters again.

ASTRID FENRIS

When I went to Kessel, the *Horizon* wasn't trying to set any speed record, so we just backtracked along the Channel and followed the Pabol Sleheyron to Ulmatra. Most pilots making a Kessel Run will do the same. Follow the Channel 20 parsecs back from Kessel and you can pick your refinery or spice purification plant: operators on Mandrine, Zerm, Injopan, and Tilurus flood space with messages offering low rates for their services. Or you can take your business to the Outer Rim, if you've got the time and know the right people.

The only problem is it takes a long time to go 20 parsecs along the Channel, and time is credits lost. That means there are always pilots looking for new paths through the Maelstrom, and bragging about secret routes only they could have been brave enough to discover — routes that will save their customers invaluable time moving spice or coaxium. Now you understand what Han did: he figured out a route through the Maelstrom that was much shorter than going back along the Channel. Everybody agrees on that much. But they want to fight about everything else.

Now, the people who run those refining operations aren't exactly the best of friends. They're constantly undercutting each other on price, badmouthing each other's business, and sabotaging each other's operations.

Things are always simmering. The Empire likes it that way, at least until things boil over and the flow of fuel and credits gets choked off. When that happens, they send in stormtroopers and Star Destroyers and everyone lies low until things get back to normal.

SPECIAL REFINERY DISCOUNTS!

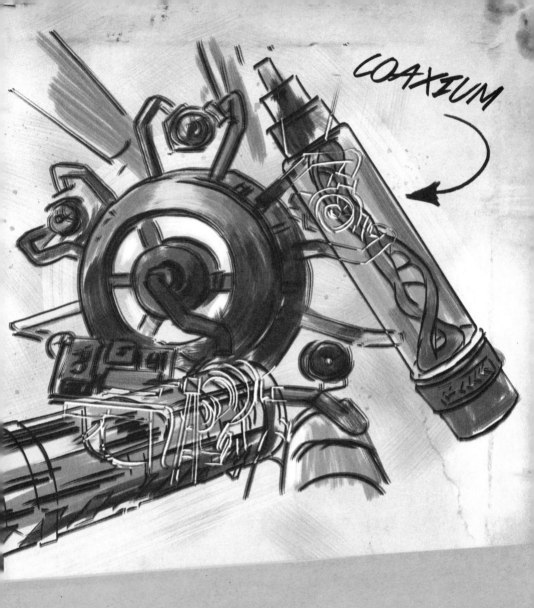

COAXIUM

So in the galactic neighborhood of Kessel you'll find lots of refineries and processing stations. Most are controlled by the Pykes through various shady dealings, but others are backed by the Hutts, the Mining Guild, or the other syndicates. Not to mention independents setting up wildcat outposts.

If spice is king on Kessel, coaxium is queen.

There's two kinds of coaxium — static and astatic. I hear the static kind forms on planets near stellar anomalies — black holes, neutron stars, and other dangerous stuff like that — but you'd have to ask a scientist about that. The point is, it's good starship fuel — which means the Empire wants it, and keeps it in well-guarded storehouses, like the one here on Vandor.

The astatic variety of coaxium is much more valuable, and as far as I know it's only found on Kessel. Mining astatic coaxium makes spice look like a picnic. First you've got to separate out the impurities. Then you've got to keep the coaxium stable until it's refined — mess up the refining process and it explodes. So the Pykes keep it in thermal vaults until a buyer has lined up a refinery and a pilot to take it there. That's what a Kessel Run is — a pilot moving coaxium or spice from the mines to the next stage of processing.

Spice also needs to be purified for sale. The Empire sharply limits how much refining of spice and coaxium can be done on Kessel itself. There are a couple of reasons for that. The first is that it would give the Pykes too much control of those markets. The second is that an accident or sabotage could set off a chain reaction that might take out a lot of the mining operations that make the Empire rich.

He said the hunters in the Dark looked like huge armored spiders, and stank like spice and rotten meat.

I've never heard anything like that about Kessel from anyone else who's been there, but Fugas was telling the truth, or at least he thought he was. There'd been something down there in the mines with him, and it terrified him. He's still a miner — he'll come in after his shift, with his new Mining Guild buddies — but he's done with spice, and Kessel, and things that want to eat you in the darkness.

FUGAS
FANDITA

That's what the veterans call the mines: the Dark. I'd been working here a few weeks when an old Gotarite spent all night in the Lodge, picking at a kod'yok steak. His name was Fugas Fandita and he had forearms like airspeeder pistons, hands that looked like stone, and a thousand-parsec stare.

Fugas told me he'd just finished a 12-year sentence on Kessel, and the Pykes had offered him a job as a shift boss. Fugas had told them no, and was looking to catch on with the Mining Guild instead. When the Pykes make an offer like that, a wise being doesn't refuse. But Fugas swore he'd never go down in the Dark again. He told me there were things down there that fed on unwary miners. Supposedly they were attracted to light and could sense motion, so the crews shut their helmet lights off and held still when they heard something in the tunnels. But Gotarites have low-light vision, and an excellent sense of smell. So Fugas could still see.

Kessel itself isn't much to look at: a rusty-looking world. One side has scrub forests, while the other is covered with open pits like sores, and choking in clouds of noxious Kessoline. Back when the royal family was in charge, gangs ran the mines and were constantly tunneling sideways to break into each other's territories and try and take them over. The Pykes put an end to claim-jumping, so you're unlikely to get caught in a mine war these days.

Instead, you'll work until you get buried in an avalanche, suffocate, or go blind. That's better, right? Spice is king on Kessel. I never saw it mined myself, but I hear it's made up of strands of crystalline fibers that run in bands through the Kesselstone. If you're careless, you'll snap the pre-spice fibers, and that'll earn you a spot on a slave ship to Zygerria, in which case you'll wish you were back on Kessel.

No matter what species you are, the mines will find a way to do you in. Heavy work gets done by Wookiees, Houks, Gigorans, Yuzzum, and other big bruiser species, but they'll put, say, a Chadra-Fan or a Ugnaught to work on more delicate tasks. Droids, too — there's plenty of jobs for mechanicals, down in the Dark.

The old-time pilots tell me it used to be different, that Kessel mined spice for medicine and other uses that actually make the galaxy a better place.

But the Pykes struck a deal with the royal family back before the end of the Republic, and then another one with the Empire that made them allies in everything but name.

WHICH KESSEL RUN?

Here's Han's most likely route. —Midnight

My navicomputer could see the gravity wells in the Maw, so it programmed a course with all these tiny twists and turns. That threw off my final heading, and all those little course corrections added up. My log showed 22 parsecs. Some shortcut, Solo!
—SONNIOD

KESSE

THE

THE CHANNE

TO ULMATRA

DA

INJOPAN

ZERM

OBA DIAH

MANDRINE

TILURUS

Han couldn't have taken the route he did — the Falcon would have been torn apart. His real route was a little different. I'll prove it next time I'm out that way. Just have to double-check a couple of calculations first.
—ASTRID

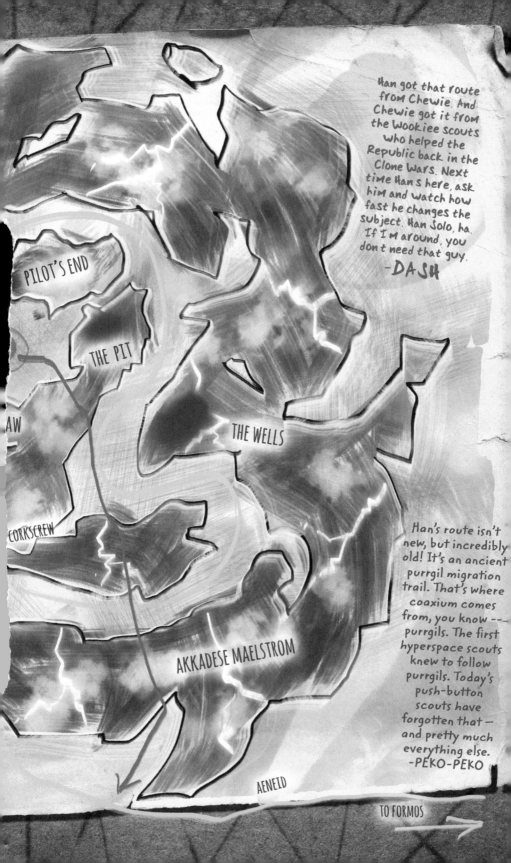

Han got that route from Chewie. And Chewie got it from the Wookiee scouts who helped the Republic back in the Clone Wars. Next time Han's here, ask him and watch how fast he changes the subject. Han Solo, ha. If I'm around, you don't need that guy.
—DASH

PILOT'S END

THE PIT

...AW

THE WELLS

CORKSCREW

Han's route isn't new, but incredibly old! It's an ancient purrgil migration trail. That's where coaxium comes from, you know —— purrgils. The first hyperspace scouts knew to follow purrgils. Today's push-button scouts have forgotten that — and pretty much everything else.
—PEKO-PEKO

AKKADESE MAELSTROM

AENEID

TO FORMOS

Those who actually get hired head into the Maelstrom along a twisting, stop-and-go route called the Channel. I take it that is how Elthree navigated Lando and Beckett's gang to Kessel in the *Falcon*.

I was up on the bridge of the *Horizon* while we were threading the Channel, and the navigator looked scared the entire time — I'd watch the beads of sweat form on her forehead, trickle down her face and roll under her uniform collar. I get it: you're hoping nothing on your ship breaks down and trusting that the data loaded into your navicomputer will be enough to keep you safe. You see, all that rock and dust and gas is always shifting around, meaning this month's safe passage may be next month's barrier. Not to mention there are pirates, slavers, and Imperial customs ships lurking and waiting for prey.

And assuming you get through unscathed, you still have to deal with the Pykes.

A ship approaching Kessel typically does so from Formos, where you'll find all sorts of smugglers waiting for charters. Or at least that's what they say they're doing.

Most of the time when a pilot says, "I'm waiting for a charter," what he really means is "I'm playing sabacc and getting into trouble."

THE KESSEL RUN

Yes indeed, keep your space adventures, thanks — your friend Midnight is staying dirtside. And even if I did want to start freighter-tramping again, I'd skip Kessel on account of it being one of the most dangerous places in the galaxy.

You'll find Kessel near the border of Hutt Space, surrounded by massive clouds of dust and gas known as the Akkadese Maelstrom. Nearby you'll find lots of hazards that wary spacers have given nicknames: the Maw, the Black Pits, Pilots' End, and other perils.

I like a good story, but if something goes wrong aboard a starship you're either trying to breathe vacuum or drifting in a tin-can escape pod and hoping somebody finds you. And there's just so much that could go wrong: every week I hear stories about pirate attacks, hyperdrive malfunctions, mynock infestations, collisions with rogue asteroids, catastrophic depressurizations, close encounters with space slugs, solar storms, fuel-line poisonings, lightspeed psychosis; and more.

I've heard stories from a lot of hot-shot pilots since Beckett's gang raided Kessel, and every single one of those pilots has an opinion on what, exactly, they did or didn't do.

Some say Han, Beckett, and Chewbacca stormed the mines. Others say Lando was the star of the battle (but that might just be Lando himself spreading those rumors). There were whispers about a droid revolution, or was it a slave uprising? I can't recall. But if you were to ask me, I bet Qi'ra was the one who took care of the Pyke Syndicates in order to get the coaxium they needed.

I've been to Kessel once myself, aboard the Horizon. Once was enough, but then I don't plan to ever leave Vandor again.

The guy walked into the Lodge as the incompetent pilot of an impounded ship, with two credits, a bunch of capes, and a winning smile. And he turned that into... well, I'm not really sure what he's turned that into. But it's a lot more than I would have guessed, that's for sure. And I like thinking that the galaxy is a place where something like that can happen.

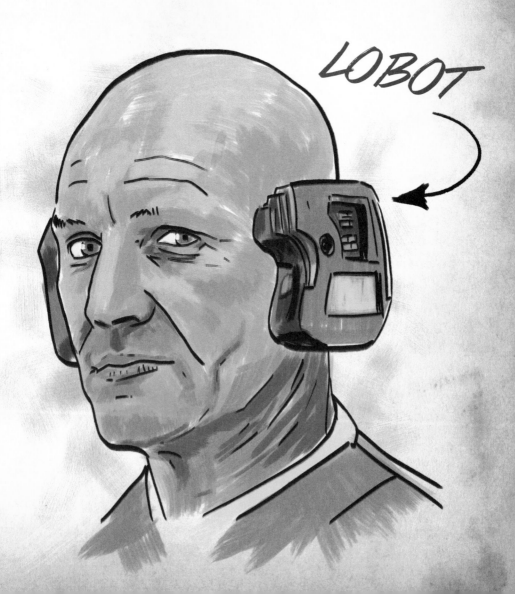

LOBOT

Shortly after that, Lando apparently lost the Falcon to Han in a sabacc game somewhere. The next time he dropped by the Lodge, he was flying a rented space yacht with a hyperdrive motivator that was always breaking down. When I asked if Han had cheated, a muscle in Lando's cheek started to twitch and he told me that he never, ever wanted to hear that name again as long as he lived.

I haven't seen Lando in a while, though every now and then I'll hear that he's conned someone out of something. These days he's got a new buddy, a fellow named Lobot who has an Imperial cybernetic construct jacked into his brain. Lobot seems the sensible sort, and Lando needs a sensible sort at his side to make him less Lando. But do you really need a tactical implant in your head to tell Lando that his latest scheme is probably a bad idea?

Last I heard, Lando and Lobot were sniffing around Cloud City. That's one of the bigger sabacc tournaments in the Outer Rim, so I can guess what they're up to. Maybe Lando will make a fortune. Maybe he'll get himself killed. I wouldn't be surprised either way. Still, I hope it goes well for him.

So anyway, Lando was hanging around the Lodge claiming he was retired while trying to win enough to settle his debts, or at least get his ship out of Tibbs's lot. Except he started living it up, which meant his stack of credits never got any bigger. In fact, it started to shrink. Then Beckett and his gang showed up, and the next thing we knew they were gone and Lando and Elthree were gone with them. And there was no sign of the *Millennium Falcon*.

When I asked Tibbs how Lando had paid his bill, he said next time he saw Lando he was going to feed him to a flock of luftgriffs. Yep, Lando had skipped out on another debt. To Lando's credit, he did come back. But Elthree didn't — Lando said she died fighting for droid rights. Lando paid Tibbs, plus a little extra for all the trouble, so the luftgriffs went hungry. But for once in his life he didn't want to talk about his adventures.

Anyway, Ralakili paid Sansizia Chreet — she's one of the droid trainers — to wire up restraining bolts with remote triggers activated by that unit he carries around with him. Every droid sent to the pits gets one, and with a click of a button Ralakili can give them a shock. Even when there isn't a fight going on, you'll catch Ralakili pushing that button, just because he can.

Tibbs doesn't care, as long as he gets his cut of the betting. But I do. The galaxy's a hard enough place as it is without people being cruel. Elthree swore that one day she'd get that remote away from Ralakili, wire him up, and see how he liked it. I'm not proud of saying it, but sometimes I wish she had.

RALAKILI

THE MAN WHO HATED DROIDS

Ralakili runs the droid pits, and trust me, friend – you want to keep away from him. He's got a mean streak like no other. I hear his planet got torched by Separatists, back in the droid war, and that's why he hates mechanicals so much. Lots of my neighbors back on Corellia felt the same way, but Ralakili takes it way too far. The droid war was a long time ago, and the droids in Ralakili's pits had nothing to do with it. Plus, if you're angry about something a droid did, you blame the programmer, not the mechanical.

So after that it was pretty common for Elthree to show up in the middle of the night to give me a droid arm or something and sit down to chat with Essvee for a while.

I never did find out why Lando sometimes called Elthree "Vuffi," though. She said it was the Socorran word for "sweetheart," while he said it was an old joke, and you had to be there.

I wouldn't necessarily call Elthree a "sweetheart." She was certainly annoying. And we didn't have much in common. But she knew what she cared about, and I respected that about her.

One thing we did agree on was Ralakili's droid fights, though...

It's not so much that I support droid rights, despite Elthree's best efforts to convince me. It just seems wasteful. Why send mechanicals out to blast, saw, or shock each other when you could sell them or break them down for wiring and components?

And the whole time Essvee is trying to get her to be quiet, because she was afraid that now she'd get unplugged.

Elthree and I struck a deal: if she didn't make trouble, she could sit at the end of the bar and keep Essvee company. Oh, and I'd collect spare protocol-droid parts so that someday someone could buy Essvee and restore her body. I don't think that's very likely — there's not much use for a protocol droid on Vandor, which is how Essvee wound up as furniture in the first place — but I didn't see the harm.

Elthree practically blew a circuit when she discovered Essvee back here with me, translating drink orders. I can still hear her like it was yesterday:

"Midnight! I thought you were one of the decent ones, but you're another meatbag! That droid is not furniture! She is a person, with her own history and hopes and dreams! You should be ashamed of yourself!"

Let me tell you a little about Elthree.

She was a pain, always interfering with the droid fights and yelling that her people had rights and weren't just property.

Ralakili wanted to dismantle Elthree, but Tibbs told him to leave her alone—I think he liked her spunk, even though we don't usually serve her kind here.

ELTHREE

DROID'S RIGHTS

— ARE SENTIENT RIGHTS

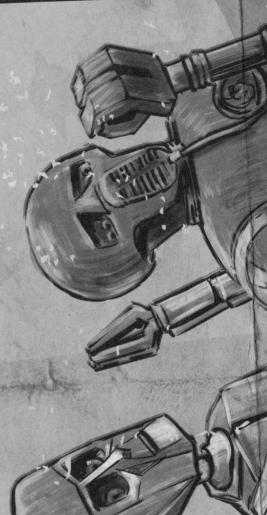

Organics! YOU ARE BETTER THAN THIS. Consider the following:

SUPPORT DROID RIGHTS! FOR A BETTER GALAXY!

Whether mechanical or organic, every sentient being is a miracle to be cherished and preserved! Droids protect you – now it's your turn to protect them!

• **The Galactic Constitution declares all sentients are equal!**
If droids lack personalities, why are memory wipes recommended to eliminate personality quirks? Mechanicals think and feel – if allowed to do so!

• **The Galactic Constitution outlaws slavery and forced servitude!**
A restraining bolt is not a fair contract! Slavery is considered an outrage to be met with the wrath of the Imperial Navy! Yet slavery goes unquestioned when its victims are made of metal and wires instead of flesh and blood!

• **The Galactic Constitution guarantees protection from hardships!**
You'd be outraged if organic workers were subjected to brutal conditions and thrown away after being injured on the job! Yet droids face such a fate every working day!

How he'd been awarded the title Savior of Livno III, wherever that is. How he found something called the Mindharp of Sharu and accidentally destroyed a star system, then defeated an evil sorcerer who dedicated his life to trying to kill him. (Nobody believed that last story, particularly when Lando let slip that the evil sorcerer could fit in the palm of your hand.)

When Lando met Han, he'd just finished a smuggling run from Felucia, and was telling everyone that he was retired — a gentleman of leisure who didn't want any trouble.

I had my doubts, so I asked Elthree. She said the *Falcon* was sitting in Tibbs's impound lot, locked down with ion restraining bolts. Turns out Lando used the wrong fake ship ID when they landed, and some folks wanted the docking fees he hadn't paid.

And sure enough, by the next night Lando had a handful of credits. Not a lot — he was still drinking plain fizz-water — but more than two. And everyone in the Lodge knew him — heck, within a week newcomers were walking in and asking me if Lando was here. He was working on business deals with half of Vandor and trying to meet the other half. He'd been aboard Dryden Vos's yacht, and out to look at a kod'yok ranch, and was talking about buying land along a potential new conveyex line.

Stories? Lando had about a million of them. How he'd been the best numbers runner and gambler on Socorro. How a disapproving father had kept him from marrying into a mining fortune on Drogheda.

YARITH BESPIN
CASINO

Welcome to sabacc at the Yarith Bespin! Tonight we're playing Corellian Spike, which adds a challenging wrinkle to the galaxy's greatest game!

Our house rules may be different than how you play back home, so here is a quick refresher:

Each sabacc game takes three rounds. Each player is dealt two cards from the deck of 62, with a third "spike" card visible to all players. Card values are positive, negative, or zero. Play proceeds left from the dealer's position, with players drawing, swapping and discarding to get as close to zero as possible – though there are better and worse ways to reach that score. Players bet, and at the end of each round the dealer rolls the dice – which can radically change your hand.

Now that you know the basics, here's a step-by-step guide to playing Corellian Spike at the Yarith Bespin:

- Each player contributes two credits to the game pot and one to the sabacc pot.

- The dealer deals two cards to each player. Players keep their cards secret, with the remaining cards placed face down as the draw pile.

- Starting from the dealer's left, players bet, see a player's bet, raise a bet, stand or decide to junk their hand, in which case their cards are discarded face up on the discard pile. A player who junks is out of the game until the next round.

- Once betting ends, the dealer deals a third card – the spike card – face up to each remaining player.

- Each player now has the option to buy a card for two credits' contribution to the game pot. The player is given the top card face down from the draw pile, after which the player may discard this card, swap it with one of the two cards in his or her hand, or swap it with the spike card.

- Players now bet again.

- The dealer rolls the dice. If the symbols are the same but not double spikes, all active players discard the two cards from their hand and are given two new cards. If double spikes are rolled, the remaining players discard all three cards and are given new cards, with the new spike card once again face up.

- Return to the option to buy a card, bet and roll the dice two more times in succession.

- If at this point more than player remains in the game, players reveal their hands. The player with the best hand wins the game pot. If the winning hand has a value of zero, that player also wins the sabacc pot.

The best winning hand is the Idiot's Array, consisting of a 0 coupled with a +2 and +3. The next best hand is the Prime Sabacc, a +10, -10 and a 0. Your Croupier droid can tell you the hierarchy of other possible winning hands, ranging from the Yee-Haa to the Nulrehk variations.

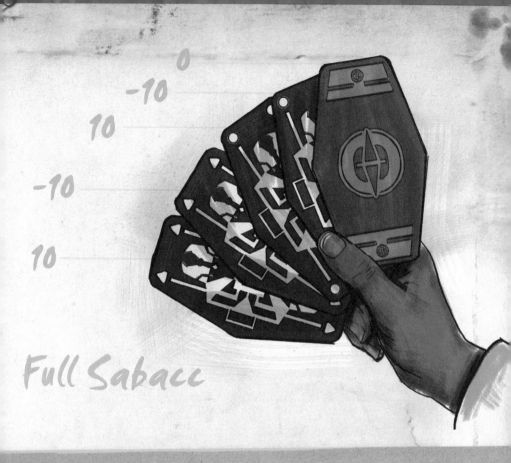

-10

0

10

-10

10

-10

10

Full Sabacc

If he'd bought the jun-lime he wouldn't have had two coins to rub together. When I mentioned this, he just grinned.

"Midnight, my man, I've got two credits and that's all Lando Calrissian needs," he said. "In half an hour I'll have four. An hour after that I'll have eight. And pretty soon you'll have another story for your collection."

Lando was at Fort Ypso because he was looking for a sabacc game—that was what he wanted and what he needed—but he was too busted to scrape together table stakes, and nobody in the back room seemed interested in acquiring a cape. I met him after he failed to get a game and retreated to the bar. He asked for a fizz-water, then frowned when I told him the fizz was free but the jun-lime wedge cost extra.

He shrugged, then savored the water like it had been brought on a platter in the fanciest restaurant on Coruscant. Lando had—and this is not an exaggeration, friend—two credits to his name.

Whenever Lando brought up his ship, the Millennium Falcon, Elthree would scoff that he couldn't fly 10 kilometers through interstellar space without finding something to crash it into.

LANDO CALRISSIAN

When I arrived on Vandor, I hadn't seen anything besides a Corellian favela, the inside of a bulk freighter, and a few third-class spaceports. I didn't know anything except how to follow orders and turn a hydrospanner. I was your basic green-as-grass kid, in other words. Which is all right — the only way to learn is by living.

Since the day I stepped off that freighter, I've seen a lot of green kids, and I've figured out they come in two varieties: those who don't know anything and know they don't, and those who don't know anything but think they do. Sometimes, though, you get someone a bit different. Someone like Lando Calrissian.

Lando showed up at the Lodge with a big smile, a remodeled YT 1300 freighter, and an impressive collection of capes — I mean, seriously, I don't think I've ever seen him wear the same one twice. Very impressive, until I started finding out more about him.

Starting with the fact that he couldn't really fly that fancy freighter of his. His pilot droid, L3-37, did that.

was Chewie's idea, because the Wookiee is apparently a leader in the Kashyyyk resistance and connected with the Rebellion. Tregga concluded that Chewie attracts a lot less Imperial attention as Han Solo's co-pilot than he would if people knew he was the brains of the operation.

Keep in mind that the sabacc players in the back room love seeing Tregga walk in because his implant calculates probabilities incorrectly and he never realizes it. So if Tregga gets that thing fixed, maybe I'll reconsider some of his crazy stories.

Speaking of Kashyyyk, one of my regulars, a smuggler named Tregga, had a crazy theory about Han Solo and Chewbacca. Granted, Tregga is kind of a strange fellow, with one of those brain implants that figures out odds for you, but he's done a few jobs with Han and Chewie, and swears Han's lying about his childhood.

According to Tregga, Han was orphaned when he was just a baby and raised by a band of wandering galactic traders. He spent most of his youth on Kashyyyk — that's where he met Chewbacca, and where he learned to speak Shyriiwook. Tregga even claims Han was on the planet when the Republic arrived to fight the Separatists, and provided the Republic generals with a clue to finding General Grievous himself. And that when the Empire took over the planet, Chewie escaped with Han and raised him, with the two of them scratching out a living on planets such as Coonee and Saberhing before running afoul of the Empire on Mimban.

When I asked why Han would lie about how he grew up, Tregga said the cover story

TREGGA

The Wookiees expected the clones to leave, but instead the soldiers got new armor and new orders. They rounded up the Wookiees, destroyed their villages, and started sawing down the giant trees.

Chewie was worried about his family—he didn't even know if they were alive. And he was angry, too. Now, I've seen an angry Wookiee, and you want to keep your distance—arms and legs tend to go flying. But this was a different kind of anger: quiet, slow-burning and impossible to extinguish. I guess you can afford to be patient when you live hundreds of years.

Mark my words, friend: Chewbacca will return to Kashyyyk one day, and when that happens a whole lot of Imperials will wish they'd been stationed somewhere else.

Chewie told me how the Republic had invaded his home planet at the very end of the droid war, to protect it from the Separatists, and Chewie and other Wookiees had fought alongside the clone troopers against Dooku's machines.

It was late and we were alone in the Lodge, so I asked Chewie if that meant he'd fought with the Jedi. He knew that was a dangerous question, and looked around before he answered, his blue eyes bright and wary. Then he told me he had — in fact, he'd fought with some of the most famous Jedi Generals, such as Yoda and Unduli. It was strange hearing those names again. It was strange even mentioning the Jedi. Chewie said the clone forces were still on Kashyyyk when the Republic became the Empire, even though there was no enemy left to fight — just shut-down battle droids.

He also said how good Lumpy was with tools and instruments – better than Chewie was at the same age. He swore Lumpy would be a great technician or pilot one day, or perhaps both, and he was just busting with pride about him. Pride – and sorrow at how rarely he got home to see him.

Chewbacca had plenty of good tales. He told me he'd been an Imperial prisoner on Mimban, kept in a muddy pit and forced to fight to entertain stormtroopers. That's how he met Han— the Empire caught him deserting and threw him into the hole. Chewie said he almost killed Han twice: once when Han was thrown into the pit and once because his attempt at speaking Shyriiwook was so terrible.

Chewie's determined to keep Han out of trouble, but mostly he wants to go home to Kashyyyk. He told me about his wife, Mallatobuck, and his son, whom I'll call Lumpy because there were a bunch of extra syllables in there that I probably didn't hear right. Chewie told me how brave Lumpy was, shaking his head about the time he sneaked away to find wasaka berries in Kashyyyk's lower forest, which is far too dangerous for a full grown Wookiee, to say nothing about a young one.

traded Tibbs a protocol droid named SV-38P who'd been on the wrong end of a bad airspeeder crash out around Jirree Town. Tibbs took Essvee's cognitive module and jacked it into the circuitry beneath the bar; wiring it to a transmitter that's connected to an earpiece I wear. That lets me tell the difference between someone saying "I'm really enjoying this fine meal and would like to leave a generous tip" and "if the guy on the next stool doesn't leave me alone I'm going to jab him with my stinger and then get rid of all the witnesses." Which is the kind of thing you definitely want to know. Poor Essvee wasn't consulted about the arrangement, but she's mostly accepted her new job, and only complains every hour or so. Most of what Essvee translates for me is just boring orders, but like me she's come to appreciate a good tale.

CHEWBACCA

One reason I have hope about Han is his friend Chewbacca. Chewbacca looks fearsome, but I soon learned that he's an old softie once you get to know him. And he has amazing stories to tell.

Chewie — I think it's okay if I call him that — is nearly 200 years old, still young for a Wookiee. Like too many members of his species, he's a refugee from his home world. The Empire has ravaged Kashyyyk, cutting down its trees for lumber and sentencing Wookiees to hard time in labor camps.

Here's a secret, friend: I speak a lot fewer languages than you'd guess watching me work. Sure, I may be standing there nodding at a Wookiee, Kyuzo or Rodian, but I don't speak any thing but Basic. A few weeks after I started working at the Lodge, someone

Now that Han's a well-known smuggler, not a week goes by without someone asking if it's true that he got his start right here in Fort Ypso.

My answer depends on who's asking.

If it's some hotshot pilot, I'll admit it and watch him and every other pilot start arguing about Kessel Runs.

If it's an underworld type, well, my memory isn't what it used to be. Han Solo? That's a funny-sounding name – you sure it's not something somebody made up?

Still, all those folks are looking in the wrong place. As far as I know, no one's seen Han on Vandor since the day the Falcon left for Kessel. I tell those folks to try Takodana, or maybe Tatooine.

Still, maybe one day Han will come back to the Lodge. If that happens I'll be eager to ask about just a few of the stories that I've heard since he left. And I'll be glad to see him.

I've seen too many smugglers, gunrunners, and outlaws working here. Most of them were people you never wanted to see again. But Han? He pretended he was one of them, but he wasn't. I knew he was a good-hearted kid who only thought of himself as an outlaw, rather than being the real thing. I hope he stayed a good-hearted kid – and that he figured out something to believe in besides himself.

I can tell if you're armed, and if you're used to being armed. A newbie walks around like the blaster on his hip weighs 10 kilos, but a veteran moves like the weight is nothing new to her.

Qi'ra carried herself like her blaster was an old friend.

And she had the manner of someone used to being obeyed. When she'd come to see me, she was always polite and professional. She never treated me or anyone else like a servant, asked for anything unreasonable, or tried to shortchange old Tibbs. But whether she needed kod'yok steaks for Vos's yacht or information about an overdue courier, Qi'ra expected to be taken seriously and dealt with quickly and fairly. She had a certain authority, I guess that's the word. The kind you'd expect from a Crimson Dawn lieutenant ... and then something more.

Qi'ra. Remember that name. Something tells me we'll all hear it again.

Anyway, Qi'ra went off with Beckett's gang, and after that ... who knows?

Let me tell you a little more about Qi'ra. She didn't exactly look fierce. Why, I doubt she'd come up to the knee joint of a bageraset. But people don't wind up with Crimson Dawn's symbol on their wrists unless they can handle themselves. And Qi'ra definitely could.

How do I know that? Because working at the Lodge, I've seen about a thousand outlaws and bounty hunters, which means I got a crash course in body language – no matter how many limbs you have or what they look like.

QI'RA

Beckett had to go crawling aboard Dryden Vos's yacht to explain what had gone wrong. Either Vos was in an exceptionally good mood or Han and Beckett worked with Vos's lieutenant Qi'ra on another plan, because next thing I heard, they had stolen a fortune in coaxium from the Pykes on Kessel, then got away with Han flying Lando Calrissian's ship, the *Millennium Falcon*.

But if you're a kid like Han, flying freighters and tugs sounds like work, not adventure. Those kids want to fly a starfighter, and imagine themselves on a recruiting poster blasting pirates and rebels. But most of them wind up flying cargo shuttles if they're lucky and talking to people flying cargo shuttles if they're not.

And if they're really unlucky, they wind up dead—they fly into an asteroid during a training exercise, or get blasted by a pirate in the Outer Rim, or meet one of a hundred other fates they don't mention on those posters.

The point is the Empire's a lousy way to see the galaxy. But it's better than dying young in Coronet City's sewers as a scrumrat.

Anyway, somehow Han and Chewbacca hooked up with Beckett's gang on Mimban to steal coaxium off an Imperial conveyex, except Val and Rio didn't make it, Han lost the shipment, and the explosion blew Luftgriff Peak clean in half.

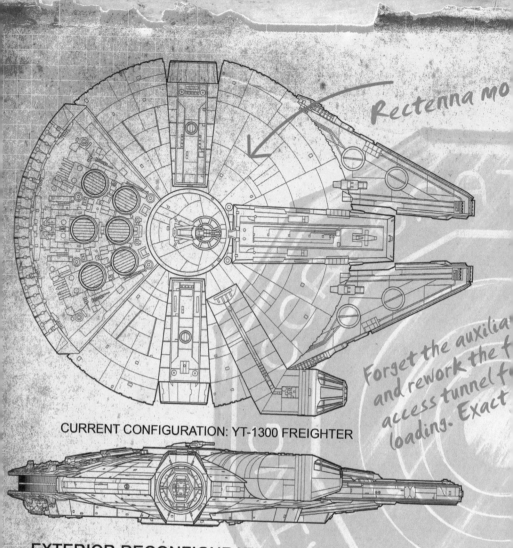

Rectenna mo

Forget the auxilia
and rework the f
access tunnel fo
loading. Exact

CURRENT CONFIGURATION: YT-1300 FREIGHTER

EXTERIOR RECONFIGURATION/REPAIR LIST:
MILLENNIUM FALCON (CEC S/N YT 492727ZED)

1 MOUNT NEW RECTENNA, DORSAL POSITION (MODEL TBD)
2 PATCH AND REINFORCE DAMAGED HULL PLATING
3 REPLACE DORSAL/VENTRAL CANNONS WITH QUAD LASERS
4 ADD QUICK-START MODS TO REPULSORLIFT/ENGINES
5 INSTALL SUBLIGHT ACCELERATION MOTOR SYSTEM
6 MOUNT CONCUSSION MISSILES IN OLD AUXILIARY CRAFT HATCH
7 RELOCATE TRACTOR BEAM PROJECTORS TO FRONT MANDIBLES
8 INSTALL SENSOR ARRAY AND ROUTE FEEDS TO RECTENNA DISH
9 ADD IDENTIFY FRIEND/FOE TRANSPONDER SUPPLIED BY CUSTOMER
10 RETROFIT GUN WELL WITH ROTATING CORE

Scrap this. IMPRACTICAL

el?

y craft
orward
r freight
specs coming soon.

ESCAPE POD: STANDARD OPTIONS

INTERIOR RECONFIGURATION PUNCH LIST:
MILLENNIUM FALCON (CEC S/N YT 492727ZED)

[SEE SEPARATE DOCUMENTATION]

Interior modifications noted and approved.

HS

(Everyone knows Corellian Engineering Corporation builds the fastest warships for the Empire. I know it's ridiculous, but I gotta admit that makes me a little proud.)

Working for CEC is a good ticket off world – but it's a ticket that's hard to get unless you've got the education, and you can't get the education unless your family has credits. And if you're a poor kid, your best bet is to win a spot in the Merchant Galactic – the top piloting jobs go to Imperial Academy kids, but you don't need an Academy diploma to rise up the ranks moving freight for the military.

MIMBAN